WORLD WAR BITCOIN

A SCENARIO OF GLOBAL ECONOMIC WAR...

Peter A. Frandano

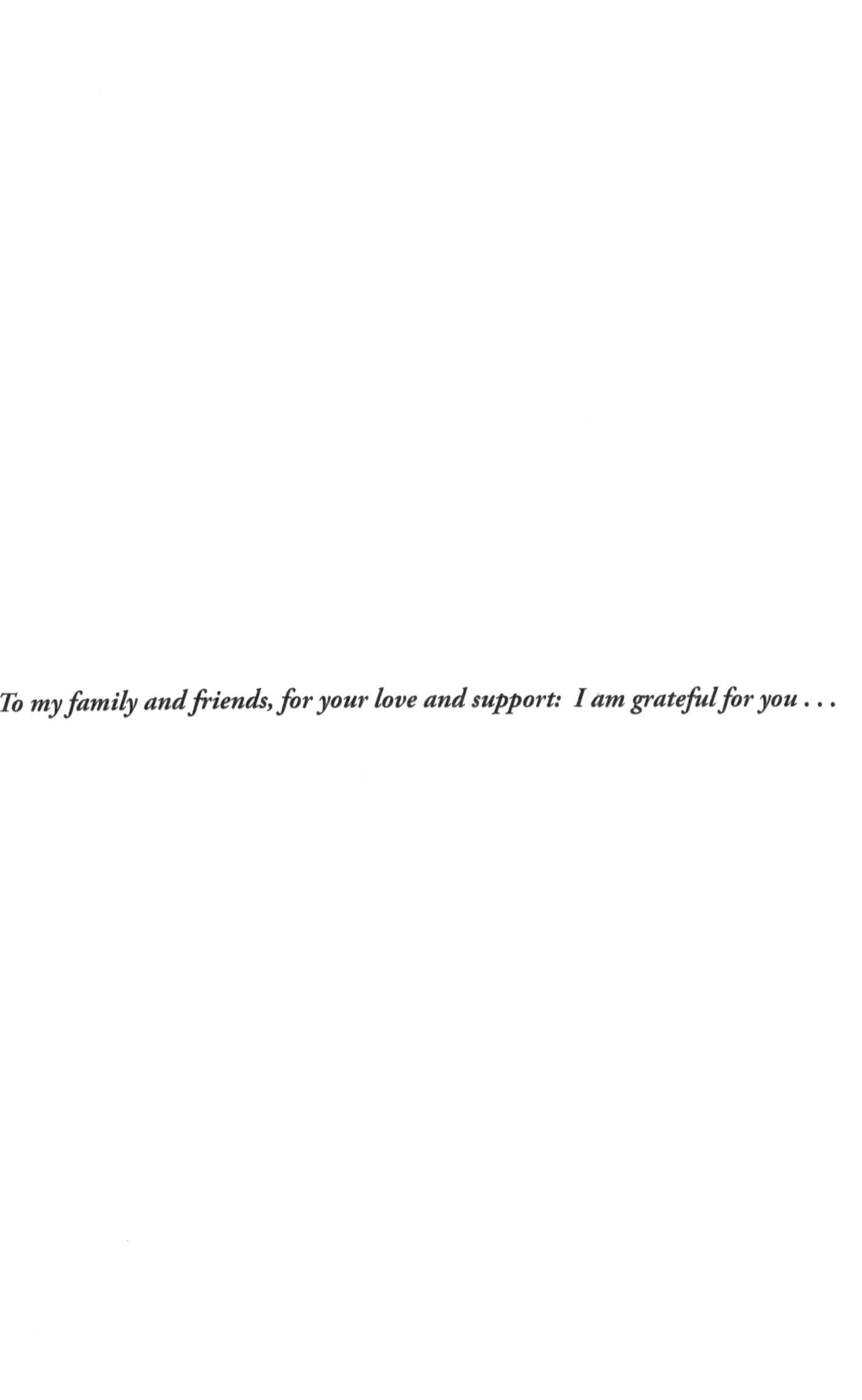

To my family and friends, for your love and support: I am grateful for you . . .

CONTENTS

INTRODUCTION

"There are decades where nothing happens, and there are weeks where
decades happen . . ."
– Vladimir Lenin

Greetings and thank you for coming on this journey with me!

The world of cryptocurrency has intrigued me for quite some time now. Though I'm certainly no fan of communist dictators, I think the quote above by Lenin is apropos when it comes to cryptocurrency.

World War Bitcoin is fiction, but it is also a forward look into what I consider to be a plausible albeit (possibly) extreme scenario in a sea of endless scenarios.

We often try to connect the dots to our experiences, grasping for something familiar. With the world of cryptocurrency similar to this pandemic we are still navigating our way out of, in my humble opinion, there is one clear similarity:

We have NEVER been here before . . .

It seems we hear the word "disruption" a lot these days. Some say, "*Disruption is coming,*" almost as a fear-inciting tactic. I respectively disagree. I say that in just about every sector of our society disruption is not one thing, it's three things. Disruption is 1) coming, 2) is here at our doorstep, and 3) is going to keep coming . . . *and that's okay!*

This book spawned from what I call my over-the-newspaper moment about eight years ago when my then 14-year-old transacted with one of his friends, one paying off a bet lost to the other using "virtual currency."

An intelligent lad, at that same early age, he was gently berating me about what he saw as the negatives of fiat currency. As someone who considers himself very fortunate to have had an amazing combined 30-year career in the Fortune 500 supply chain and real estate arenas, well, let us just say it caused me to raise my eyebrow . . . My son was teaching me.

Do I now consider myself a cryptocurrency expert? Far from it!

One of many important things I have learned along my journey: sometimes we have to take a leap of faith on the advice and counsel of others who happen to be smarter or more knowledgeable than we are on a certain topic. In this arena, many know a lot more than I will ever know and I love that! I'm constantly learning . . .

My goal with this book is certainly not to predict the direction or trajectory of Bitcoin (BTC). I wanted to have fun authoring a short story (technically a "novelette", that category between short story and novel); I also wanted to open minds (including my own) and to force myself and hopefully others to dive deeper into the "what" that is going on behind the scenes. Similar to the "what" that was happening behind the scenes on Wall Street and in the hallways and backrooms of our governments around the globe prior to the Great Recession.

In *World War Bitcoin*, I highlight four world powers: the United States, China, Russia and North Korea. Of course, there are other countries and entities currently playing in this world, but in our story, I stick with these four.

A note on names of either characters or companies: this story, the characters and the entities are fiction. My intent is not to harm or slander. For instance, you might see a government leader mentioned and think "hey, that is not her real name?!" Well, that is because I have changed it here. You will certainly see some facts and real places mixed in for good measure. If I cite a source, I have tried to note it. You will notice a few endnotes of what I believe are interesting articles or sources that were relevant. Information that helped me round out my understanding and thinking. There were many more articles and sources used; I only cite a few here if I used them to help enhance the book.

Why the title, *World War Bitcoin*? I am not a conspiracy theorist, but I do believe at times there is sleight of hand or misdirection at play, especially when it comes to a firm's bottom line or a country's national security interests. Not all is as it seems . . .

So, there you have one of the key premises of this book.

I have asked myself: what is really going on in this world of cryptocurrency? In board rooms? Behind the doors, down the halls and in the anti-chambers of governments when it comes to the topic of Bitcoin or cryptocurrency in general?

This has been a fun ride and an ongoing one as I consider myself a life-long student. The world of cryptocurrency is in its infancy stage, and I believe it will be evolutionary and transformational.

I realize Bitcoin could go to zero or over the moon and beyond. Whatever it does, I do believe this cryptocurrency moment, similar to the internet, supply chain evolution and other historic technological curve shifting events is a transformative one.

If this book causes you or someone in your world to think in a way that begets a positive change in your life and benefits your journey, I will deem it a success!

My investment disclaimer: I do not give investment advice. This book is by no means a suggestion for you to purchase Bitcoin or any other cryptocurrency nor is it a suggestion for you to not invest in them. As always, before making any investment decision, please consult your trusted advisors, do your own in-depth and thorough due diligence and research and chart your own course.

With that, I wish you strength and endurance in your valleys and your uphill climbs and a life filled with awesome peaks and crossed finish lines . . .

All my best to you and yours and Godspeed on your journey!

Pete Frandano

CHAPTER 1

SOMETHING WICKED THIS WAY COMES – RAY BRADBURY, 1962: BOSTON, MA

SEPTEMBER 11, 2001

The clock radio chimed on at 5 am to the sound of Jimmy Buffett's "Margaritaville." Anthony Romano rolled over and slapped the snooze button and rolled back over for ten more glorious minutes of snoozing. He thought about the day ahead. *Ahhh . . .*

Tom's Sporting Goods, Pittsburgh, PA . . . *Here I come*, he thought. There and back the same day to meet with Tom's Sporting Goods VP of Logistics and team to discuss what his firm, Avery Jenson, a supply chain firm focused on bar-coded products could do for them and their supply chain. Logan Airport down to Pittsburgh and back. Slam dunk! Tom's was a good customer of theirs and he was looking forward to the meeting.

Anthony popped up, turned the clock radio off, carried out his normal routine, tossed on his running shorts, shirt and shoes, went down to the lobby of the Crown Plaza hotel and out into the cool air.

It was a beautiful fall morning in Natick, Mass. The supply chain division Anthony manages is headquartered here. His family lives in Greensboro, NC. This is the life they live. He got in his quick 5K, 19 minutes or so to get his heart pumping, hopped the elevator up to the concierge level, had a tiny breakfast and was off and running.

He had an 8:45 am flight to Pittsburgh to catch . . .

Traffic was normal as he took the Logan Express. He got to the airport in his usual one hour before departure time and skipped right through the very light security. No bags to check, easy-peasy.

8

The gate attendant started calling for boarding around 8:15 am. All passengers got seated and situated and took off a few minutes later. There were only about twenty or so passengers on that USAir flight that morning—a Boeing 737—plenty of room. He could stretch out and make himself at home.

All passengers had their own row, so everyone just spread out.

As they took off, Anthony watched Boston from above, they circled the city, headed southwest toward New York, and then what would be a final zig and then a downward zag into Pittsburgh. He looked out over the wing, then shook himself out of his trance and caught up on a few white papers and downloaded emails on his laptop.

About 25 minutes into the flight, the plane intercom crackled, and the Captain came on.

"Ladies and gentlemen, good morning. Well, this is a strange one and I don't want to concern you, but ground control has issued a security alert and has requested us to reroute to Rochester, so that is what we are going to do. I don't have any more information than that. This is a new one for us . . . We're very sorry for the inconvenience but we'll get back with an update as soon as we know more."

When you are on a plane above 20,000 feet and your pilot comes over the intercom and says, "I don't want to concern you . . ." you get concerned.

Security alert? As much as Anthony was flying, and it was almost every week for quite a few years now, he had heard every excuse in the book, from mechanical, to electrical, to animal (yes, animal) to you name it . . .

Anthony had never heard the term 'security alert' when flying before. It shook him a bit. He could feel himself flush as he glanced out the window at the wing. Whew! Still intact. He had read way too many Tom Clancy novels, so his mind started racing. He looked up at the flight attendant and mouthed "security alert?" with brows arched. She looked back, eyes wide open, shaking her head, shrugging and mouthed back "I don't know."

A few minutes later, Romano heard the pilot click on the intercom again.

"Okay, good! Here comes the explanation, all a simple mistake no doubt, *let's get on down to Pittsburgh folks.*"

The pilot's voice now had a sense of urgency, almost a sweat-like quality to it. Anthony could feel the pilot's palms perspiring and now Anthony's were too.

"Okay, ladies and gentlemen, ground control has come back to us, and they want us on the ground now, so we are diverting to Syracuse. Again, no explanation other than a security alert. I can assure you that our plane is just fine. We just don't have a clue what's going on down below, so Syracuse, here we come. Flight attendants, please prepare the cabin for arrival. We are going to be going down a bit quicker than normal."

A bit quicker than normal . . .

At this point, Anthony is about to crap his pants, pulling his seat belt tighter, closing up his laptop, and stuffing all of it back in his bag. If you look at the map, Syracuse is, in fact, closer to Boston than Rochester, but not by much.

Wow! Anthony thought, *they really do want us down.*

The twenty or so folks on the plane are chatting a bit nervously, trying to keep it light, making small talk and speculating as to what could be going on.

A nuclear bomb maybe gone off somewhere? The wings on our plane are intact so that's good. Who knows?

Anthony looks out to see the ground of upstate New York rapidly approaching, and then—touchdown. At that point, cell phones start to flip on. A fairly quick taxi to the gate, seatbelt "ding" goes off, and everyone jumps up from their seats to begin collecting their stuff.

Anthony was scurrying down the aisle when his office assistant, Norma calls in . . .

In her sweet southern drawl, she says, "Good Lord, Anthony, I'm so glad you are okay! Kim wanted me to check in on you . . . Are you okay?"

"Yes, Norma, I'm fine, but what the heck is going on?"

"We're not sure but the news said all planes in the continental U.S. are being grounded due to a small plane—they called it a "Cessna"—hitting one of the World Trade Center towers and they are taking precautions all over the country . . ."

Most of Anthony's colleagues knew he was flying out of Boston that morning. He had no idea that at this point they were concerned he was 'toast,' but yes, concerned they were.

The airport staff shuttled everyone quickly off the plane and herded the predominantly business traveling crowd like cattle down to the main concourse.

USAir Club, here I come, he's thinking. *I'll rebook, catch another plane and get down to Pittsburgh, late for my meeting but at least making the effort.*

When he arrived at the USAir Club door, it is closed. Airport and USAir staff are all waving everyone ahead like parking lot attendants—shaking their heads anticipating the question. They did not know . . . No one did.

Keep moving, folks! Keep moving was the look received.

By this time, a second plane had hit the towers and there was now speculation that the planes had originated from Boston. Anthony would later learn that they had gotten an 'early divert' or security alert message to divert and that all U.S. airspace was officially cleared by 9:45 a.m.

His phone rang again, this time it was his wife, Jenny. She had gotten through to him as he was being herded through the airport.

Flustered, Anthony told her briefly what had happened. By then, he had almost arrived at the main concourse level of the Syracuse airport, realizing now getting to Pittsburgh is probably not in his immediate future.

Jenny asked what he was going to do, and he said, "I don't know, maybe get a room here?"

Anthony was not thinking clearly and was a bit dazed. Jenny countered, suggesting an attempt at a rental car with the goal of returning to Boston.

He took her advice and angled quickly for the rental car area but when he rounded the corner, he saw what looked like a two-mile-long line of people waiting to rent cars. Promising idea. Others were obviously in the same boat.

Feeling his blood pressure starting to elevate, he hears an angel cry out: "Is anybody going to Worcester?" It was belted out in a very thick New England accent and sounded more like 'WUSTA!' but he got it. Anthony knew there was a Worcester, MA, but did not know if there was a Worcester, NY.

At that moment, as though he is in a game show, where the last person to throw their hand up or bang on the buzzer loses, Romano shot his hand up with a hopeful yet uncomfortable smile on his face, giving her the 'I'm in!' look.

The New England angel's name was Linda, a GSA employee who was in the same situation he was. She was also taking off out of Logan that morning on a different plane heading to Washington, DC. David was also in a similar boat on the same flight as Linda, and finally Peter, in the same boat also, heading to Texas. Linda had procured a four-seater and knowing others would need help, yelled out her charitable question.

Anthony, David and Peter—all took her up on it. Four complete strangers getting ready to drive across upstate New York, who by the end of that very long and lonesome day, would no longer be strangers.

When Anthony got back to his hotel in Natick that evening and began to do the dreaded deep thinking, well, that basically spelled the beginning of the end of his time in the corporate world. He had lost his cousin who was like a brother to him earlier in the year in a cycling accident in Jackson, Wyoming and at the ripe age of 33, was now suffering from a major dose of 'life is short' syndrome.

He left soon after to pursue his small business ownership dreams in the world of commercial real estate, relocating his family to beautiful Southport, North Carolina which, upon his due diligence, reminded him of Maine without the winters.

Anthony was fortunate to proceed up the curve quickly in the real estate industry, eventually purchasing the company he joined but like so many, getting crushed in the Great Recession, almost losing everything as the market got flushed down the drain.

Little Joey Romano saw his mom and dad struggle. He knew something was wrong, but he and his little brother were always sheltered from 'it.' They would hear their dad crying softly at times in his bedroom. Anthony poured all of his investments; his impressive nest egg accumulated from his time in the corporate world back into the company he had purchased in an effort to prop it up. It was a valiant attempt . . .

Romano, though grateful he had left the everyday airport scene of the corporate world he lived in, often wondered, *what have I done to my family?*

He also wondered, *what if* he had remained? The upsides for taking what he called his 'right turn' in his life were significant: he would not have been there to coach Joey's teams and be there for his two sons as they were growing up; one of his greatest fears was missing the father-son experience. But he also guessed they would be much better off financially had he not left his corporate cocoon.

What ifs. *Water under the bridge . . .* he thought.

Though he definitely knew it was his tree, he was sitting in it with no one to blame but himself; his was a too often true story of the impact of the world of backroom high finance, the Wall Street impact on main street. Anthony had once heard the former Federal Reserve Chairman, Ben Bernanke describe it this way when watching him on the news at Congressional hearings in an attempt to reverse engineer the 'why' of what had happened:

"September and October of 2008 was the worst financial crisis in global history, including the Great Depression."

To say little Joey was angry about the hurt he saw his parents going through would be a tremendous understatement.

It became what drove him in the years ahead.

A NEW DAY: HONG KONG

John Dano, awarding-winning journalist for *the World Business Journal* put the white paper down . . .

By now, Dano had pieced together that Satoshi Nakamoto, the brains behind and the creator of Bitcoin (BTC) was a student and a fan of Albert Einstein. He was an adoring fan of Carl Menger, the Austrian Economist who was widely considered the father of the *Subjective Theory of Value* and the author of the book *Principles of Economics* published in 1871. Nakamoto was also an enthusiastic fan of chemists Otto Hahn, Fritz Strassmann and physicists Lise Meitner and Otto Robert Frisch— the team who discovered nuclear fission on that glorious day in December of 1938. Nakamoto studied another of Menger's books, *On the Origins of Money,* published 21 years after *Principles of Economics.*

It had been over 12 years since the Genesis block was unleashed.

Nakamoto knew beyond any doubt that what he was creating was on par with nuclear fission and would set off a chain nuclear reaction-type event in the world of global economics and finance.

Dano had read and reread the white paper, a 9-page document[1]:

Bitcoin: A Peer-to-Peer Electronic Cash System

Satoshi Nakamoto
satoshin@gmx.com
www.bitcoin.org

Rumors swirled around the persona and whereabouts of Satoshi Nakamoto. From Elvis-like sightings to 'he's not one person but a brilliant brain trust,' to everything in between.

Dano had also by luck wandered upon a source provided to him by a friend, who confirmed Nakamoto's existence and where he lived.

The World Business Journal has three primary offices: New York, Hong Kong and

London and Dano bounced around to all three and everywhere in between as was necessary in his role.

Through his meticulous and quiet research, Dano located the property manager who managed the building in Hong Kong where Nakamoto supposedly resided. With the assistance of 10 very crisp Benjamins (he would have paid in Hong Kong dollars but too bulky and the U.S. dollar was accepted with no issues there), he was granted quiet access for about 30 minutes late one evening when most people had gone to sleep.

The apartment was untouched. The bed was made perfectly—almost with military precision—as if whoever made it was concerned about a pending senior officer inspection. It seemed as if the occupier of the apartment was planning a return. A tiny light underneath the stove vent and a small flat-screen Samsung in the second bedroom were still on, the TV tuned to CNBC. Dano knew that Nakamoto made it a practice of intently studying what the 'other side' was up to.

From the balcony, the view of the city from Victoria Peak out to Victoria Harbour (Dano's hotel, the Excelsior Hotel was down below and right on the harbor) was like no other in the world. Dano loathed what he had seen the Chinese do to this great city. Of course, when it was turned over from the British to the Chinese on July 1, 1997, ending 156 years of British rule and becoming a 'special administrative region of China,' Dano and others had a distinctly sick feeling regarding the direction Hong Kong would take once under formal Chinese rule. It did not take long for the Chinese to start quietly squeezing the life out of the goose that laid the golden eggs. 'One country, two systems' . . . *Hogwash.*

On the mahogany desk, a full copy of the 9-page white paper (stapled perfectly in the upper left corner of the pages), a copy of Carl Menger's *The Origins of Money* barely touching the upper left corner of the white paper, centered with a handwritten note immediately underneath it that simply stated:

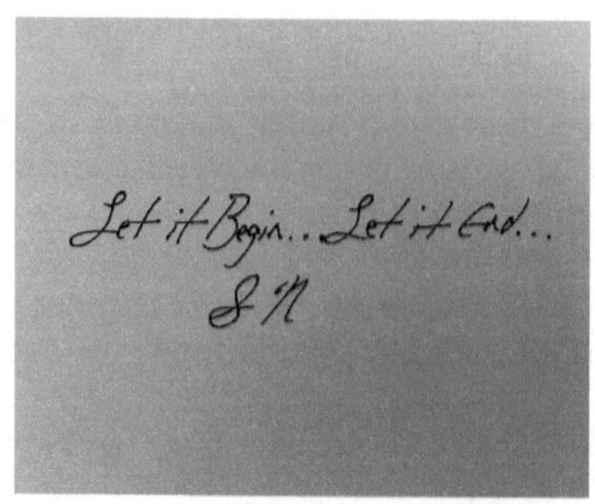

The high-end Montblanc PIX black ballpoint pen was laid in perfect horizontal fashion underneath the handwritten note, almost as if an underline for emphasis.

The room had quiet Caribbean music playing on the Sonos sound system, a lava rock was in operation with low-level lighting and a hint of coconut in the air. If you closed your eyes, you may have thought you were in a very 'chill' section of Miami's South Beach. The apartment had a high-end, clean, modern feel. No remote controls, everything seemed to be voice-controlled as Dano experimented with the TV, sound devices, lighting, all of it, and all reacted on cue. Everything was in order, perfectly arranged and perfectly serene.

One lone picture of Nakamoto with an attractive female sat on an end table touching the modern sofa. The couple was young (Dano guessed upper 20s to early 30s). Smiling, arm in arm, they looked very happy together. Both looked to be of Asian descent.

By now, Dano had spent so much time piecing information together, researching, seeking to understand the pure genius, drive and motivation of Nakamoto, he felt as if they were kindred spirits.

He could see the 'hero complex' in Nakamoto, the want and need to make a positive difference in the world for everyone. What Nakamoto had done was well beyond money, income, fame or fortune.

He was driven by what he knew was right and the defeat of what he saw as the evil powers that be: overreaching governments, overreaching corporations, overreaching individuals who had risen due to what he saw was a bankrupt and corrupt system. It was clear one of Nakamoto's top loathings: incompetent, dull witted and corrupt politicians or government officials who pretended that the greater good for all was their motivation, when in fact he knew that for them, maintaining power no matter the means was always the end game.

A couple of governments came to mind clearly when he thought of this but all governments, because they were human and humans were, well, human, could at times fall into this category. Regarding governments, there was not much he admired, but he did respect the founding fathers of the United States for at least attempting to 'check' this drive for unchecked power, although he at times questioned how well the U.S. was doing with *that*. The lowest common denominator always seemed to find a way around.

With each passing day, Dano was more firmly convinced of Satoshi Nakamoto's absolute and pure brilliance.

An anonymous Einstein of the 21st century. A revolutionary in modern times.

The comparison was there, the analogy held: Einstein was the father of physics and the nuclear weapon.

Nakamoto is the 'father' of the economic system's nuclear weapon, which is to say, the financial system as we know its demise.

Dano speculated that Nakamoto knew he had to create his work under the cover of night. That once discovered, it would make many of the sovereign powers around the globe, including the ruthless, dictatorial regimes turn and raise their collective eyebrows.

It was evident to Dano that Nakamoto understood human and sovereign nature and the need by some to maintain absolute control and power. Those sovereign entities would stop at nothing to snuff it out as quickly as possible and by any means.

Einstein: E=MC^2. Energy is equal to Mass times the speed of light squared. Dano had researched this as well to help with his hunch on the connection. The three most significant meanings of that *simple equation:*[2]

1) Even masses at rest have an energy inherent to them.
2) Mass can be converted into pure energy.
3) Energy can be used to make mass out of nothing…except pure energy.

Einstein wanted to avoid the catastrophic accelerated chain reaction.

The nuclear reaction process goes something like this: a neutron collides into the nucleus of an atom and splits it . . .

Fission occurs when a neutron strikes the nucleus of either isotope, splitting the nucleus into fragments and releasing a tremendous amount of energy. The fission process becomes self-sustaining as neutrons produced by the splitting of an atom striking nearby nuclei and produce fission.

Blockchain, and more so Bitcoin can be thought of as economic fission: a splitting apart of the economic system's atoms . . .

Enter The Genesis Block . . . the self-sustaining economic chain reaction had begun.

Genesis Block defined:[3]
On January 3, 2009, the first event on the Bitcoin blockchain occurred. Its founder, Satoshi Nakamoto placed an important notation indicating the intent behind what he had

just created. The London Times ran a cover story entitled "Chancellor on Brink of Second Bailout for Banks." This title was quoted and embedded into the very first transaction ever in the new Bitcoin blockchain by Satoshi Nakamoto.

Never forget the true meaning of Bitcoin:

Ending the control of banks and governments over your money . . .

The ultimate economic atom had been split, the pin pulled from the grenade, the genie released from the bottle and there was no putting her enraged specter back in. The 'short' of the entire financial system was on . . .

Nakamoto had essentially flipped the middle finger to the entire economic system with a nod to the commoners and a double middle finger to the controlling dictators around the world. These regimes crave complete economic control. Bitcoin is about freedom. Dano knew that this is why crackdowns had already begun in certain countries around the globe.

Yes, Dano had read Nakamoto's white paper countless times with deep fascination, certainly not understanding all of it, but he understood he was reading rare genius. As it would be difficult to pry inside the mind of Albert Einstein, so too would it be difficult to do the same with Nakamoto's. The light came on one day for Dano and he smiled, realizing what Nakamoto was up to when he unleashed The Genesis Block on the world.

Nakamoto was pure science, more specifically: pure computer science; a mathematical genius on par with Einstein and all of the other great math thinkers in world history, a blend of physicist, chemist, psychologist, brilliant financier, brilliant finance minister—all rolled into one.

Dano had heard several people over the last few months like Mark Yachtsman, President and Founder of StratagemMicro and Joe Vernon a popular host on a morning business program both who happened to be MIT alums, say in their own way: "Bitcoin is math and math doesn't lie. It cannot be manipulated, spun or twisted for one's own agenda." He had also heard Bitcoin referred to as 'perfect digital gold.' Dano got it now and they were right.

Nakamoto knew this better than anyone. He created it to be so.

Dano's phone rang—the caller ID said 'MY'; it was Michael Yachtsman.

Dano made a comment about the hypocrisy of the U.S. Treasury Secretary who had publicly voiced earlier in the day her concerns about "Cryptocurrency being an enabler of money laundering . . ."

He queried to Yachtsman: "Like it doesn't happen every day with fiat currency, right under their nose??"

Dano interviewed Yachtsman off the record just a few weeks earlier for a story on the future of Bitcoin and the "why" behind his company's significant accumulation of BTC. Dano learned from his interview that StrategemMicro has a simple litmus test[4] for Bitcoin (or any cryptocurrency) that consists of three very basic questions:

1) Can it be banned?
2) Can it be hacked?
3) Can it be copied?

Yachtsman argued convincingly that he and his team believe strongly that the answer to all three of those questions is a resounding "no" and in the world of cryptocurrency, BTC is the only one that passes the test. Therefore, Yachtsman's openly stated goal was to accumulate as much BTC as legally possible within their corporate governance. Yachtsman's unstated goal was to do it before "the Giants" (his term for government entities) pivoted and began to crowd out the market, given, unlike other "currencies," there is a finite supply of BTC. Yachtsman believes in his heart of hearts that BTC will become the world's first digital reserve currency. Some actually believe it could usurp the U.S. dollar as the world's reserve currency.

Yachtsman told Dano during the interview: "As you know, 21,000,000 individual bitcoins will be all that is ever produced. To date, there have been approximately 18.75 million bitcoins mined. Current estimates are that the final bitcoin will be mined by February 2140. So, it truly is a foot race to the finish. When the Giants pivot, and finally make their full run on BTC, and they will, the party is over for those of us in the private sector. No way we can compete . . ."

Dano and Yachtsman were careful about what they said each knowing their conversations were now being tracked.

"The good Secretary has some nerve . . ." Dano said.

She takes us as pure fools he thought.

This is what happens to Monarchs (or folks who fancy themselves Monarchs) when they suddenly wake up and feel they are more intelligent than the general populous they are lording over . . . see the French Revolution as a prime example of what happens to those Monarchs once the people catch on.

Leaders have a fiduciary responsibility to the people they are leading—a solemn oath of office.

To Dano and Yachtsman, it was obvious the Secretary's language was a veiled attempt to throw the general public and the main competitors of the U.S. off the trail of what the U.S. Treasury was truly up to.

Even well-respected individuals in the private sector, people like Jamie Platinum of JP Gorman Bank and Charlie Hunger of Brookshire Bathaway had taken swipes at BTC—with Platinum trashing it then later realizing he had to jump on board, and Hunger calling Bitcoin a "threat to civilization," akin to "snake poison." Dano knew Hunger meant a threat to *his* version of civilization. Many in power, either in prominent financial institutions or governments viewed it as a threat and were mortally afraid of it.

A more likely scenario: they were positioning and quietly accumulating it.

The private market train was leaving the station as evidenced by the adoption rate, so the public market government train knew it had to make big moves and soon; maybe even try and blow up the stations or the tracks.

Dano knew the private market train always finds other tracks. Once the train achieved maximum speed there was no stopping it.

The proverbial 'we' had walked into the room and did not spot the sucker, because the joke was on all of us. *We were the suckers . . . and Nakamoto had played us.* At this thought, Dano chuckled then sheepishly looked around to see if anyone was staring at him, even though he knew he was alone.

By the time most finance ministers, world powers, financiers, U.S. Federal Reserve Chairman, U.S. Treasury Secretary, heads of the world's prominent Intelligence agencies, heads of state, and other central bankers around the globe began to see the sun coming up on the horizon as to 'what this thing actually is and what it means,' Nakamoto had already exited the room and set the timer for the ultimate world economic detonation . . .

3 . . . 2 . . . 1 . . . Kaboom . . . a quiet, seemingly gentle version of the Big Bang theory ensued.

Too late . . . Game on.

CHAPTER 3

HEADING TO THE U.S. IN SEARCH OF ANSWERS: DEPARTING HONG KONG

It made absolute sense to John Dano that Nakamoto would make this oasis of economic freedom his home for a while. The irony did not get by him that Nakamoto had fled this place as the communist party was overrunning it, slipping the noose again, always, one step ahead.

Dano thought: *That's really what Bitcoin is, isn't it? Slipping the noose . . . one step ahead; check and mate; end around . . . ?*

Quietly clicking the door closed behind him, he walked with purpose out of the apartment and was headed to Chek Lap Kok International Airport to board a long flight, over the North Pole on Cathay Pacific.

He recalled a dear friend once telling him of Hong Kong before he made his first ever trip that the view coming in on the train was breathtaking. A nighttime arrival was always best, and it always reminded him of New York City with a mountain backdrop. His friend was not too far off.

Shaking the daydream off, he pulled out his boarding pass . . . Dano had a bit of nosing around to do in NYC and a little hardball to play...

CHAPTER 4

JOEY AND A LITTLE LUCK: SOUTHPORT, NORTH CAROLINA

As little Joey Romano grew older, he developed a bent for technology.

In 2011, when Joey was about 12, Anthony Romano had his first glimpse of the future. He watched Joey and his friend Josiah banter back and forth about a bet lost. Josiah paid Joey with something called 'Bitcoin.' Upon inquiry, the boys told Anthony that "there was no physical exchange . . . it just happened through a transfer of information . . ." They also went on to enlighten Anthony about this fascinating concept called 'Venmo.'

Little Joey had learned about Bitcoin, and he wanted one. He was driven to own one. He would shuffle back and forth on his feet, as if doing the Texas two-step, thinking day and night about how to cobble enough of the $25 he could muster to own an entire coin—not understanding yet at the time he could own a very small fractional slice of one, even one percent. So, through arduous work like mowing several neighbors' grass and other industrious endeavors, he did in fact manage to cobble enough to gobble up one entire coin, and then eventually another and then another.

He also convinced his father after lecturing dear old dad on the evils of 'fiat currency' to purchase a Bitcoin. So, for fun, Romano waded into the crypto world to appease his son. It was serious to Joey. Romano purchased several coins, taking what he called a 'fun, throwaway position.' In the coming years, he would come to realize what a blessing it was on that fateful day he gave in to his son.

Romano thought, *I do not deserve such joy as this . . .*

His son had convinced him to buy a few coins at $25 so he bought 10 of them . . .

Then he grew his little portfolio to around 70 coins with a $2,000 tax refund check he had received thinking, *Why not take a chance on the home run? The S&P 500 will never get me there . . .*

When the real estate market went under, he lost almost everything. His coins were now worth roughly $2.5 million.

Some are lucky he thought, *why not me?*

The *fun, throwaway position* he had taken on his young son's advice more than made up for his losses and the beating he took from his beloved real estate industry. Romano squinted as he watched the sun come up over the Cape Fear River one morning while sipping his coffee. He was forever grateful.

Thank you, Mr. Nakamoto, whoever or whatever and wherever you are.

He could not believe it, but it was true.

Little did Anthony know, the exponential climb up had only just begun.

Well north of him, about 6 hours and 34 mins or 397 miles to be exact, in a place often referred to as 'The District' as well as other places across the oceans, and around the globe, there were some with much larger aspirations. Very large, national security-type aspirations. Their data scientists and others were watching and analyzing BTC, day and night.

They knew about this exponential climb, sensed what was on the horizon, what was at stake and were preparing to play for keeps.

CHAPTER 5

HUNTING NAKAMOTO: THE PENTAGON – WASHINGTON, DC

Tom Jansen blew out of the ivory-colored room on the fourth floor of the Pentagon, made such a hard left turn that his Cole Haan shoes squeaked on the shiny marble floors. Walking rapidly down the hall, head down, occasionally glancing up and ahead to make sure he did not smash into someone, he could not believe what he had just heard, and he was trying to process it.

In his very long tenure in both Intelligence and Defense, the U.S. of course had ordered 'hits' before on leaders or terrorists that threatened the United States' national security interests. But to his knowledge and recollection, the United States of America had never planned the assassination of a *cyber genius* who apparently resided in another country. Rubbed up against them? Yes. Put heat on them? Of course. But assassinate? No, *never* . . .

One faction at Langley (CIA HQ) and the Pentagon wanted to find and abduct Nakamoto to bring him to safe harbor. One group of political hawks wanted him eliminated. Tom agreed with the former. His work had just begun but he felt keeping him alive and safe once found would do the world better.

That would be his goal.

CHAPTER 6

THE HAIL MARY PASS, A FIGHT FOR SURVIVAL: THE KREMLIN

Tverskoy District – Moscow, Russia

Sergey Menginov, the Russian Finance Minister, with his crusty 71-year-old shell loves his country. To this day, he is still bitter over the breakup of the former Soviet Union and the power that left with it when it was broken up into what he now thought were irrelevant and marginalized pieces.

Over the last decade or so, Sergey was sickened by the decline of his 'Mother Russian' and its currency, the Ruble.

Sergey knew intuitively what remained of his beloved country was in trouble. *Deep trouble.*

This meant he and his leadership comrades were in trouble.

The Russian people were slowly starving and at a certain inflection point, as history had proven, they would rise up against the leadership who had driven them to this precipice.

It is simply what a populace does; if you look deep into the history books, a starving people will usually eventually dispense or dispose of their inconvenient and incompetent leadership by whatever means necessary and usually, it is not pretty.

On this Wednesday morning, Sergey was fuming over the headlines: he had tuned into Sputnik News and saw that this Michael Yachtsman, a corporate executive who he learned was CEO of a U.S. based company called *StratagemMicro*, was boasting about his billion and a half dollar Bitcoin purchase. Competition for Sergey.

What made Sergey angrier is that he and his Russian comrades were so late to the party. They had missed the initial departure in a big way. He belatedly accepted this 'currency' which he now acknowledged as both a threat and an avenue of survival for the Russians, albeit admittedly without full understanding.

He also loathed the repeated beratings by his boss, Alexei Turgenev, affectionately known as *Alex*, who would bellow to him repeatedly about their Global Directorate Cyber Intelligence Team:

"Listen to them, Sergey!! They are not as stupid on such things as you and I are . . . *especially YOU!!*" and Alex would then laugh his deep and evil laugh . . . Turgenev saw something in this new currency. He felt power and control, both of which he dearly loved. Sergey knew his boss was overcome by the need for both.

Alex went on: "Look at our Asian comrades. The Chinese are cracking down on this BTC because they are afraid of it, hiding behind their usual *for the good of the people* rhetoric. They see it as a threat to their hold on their people and their currency. We have been under the thumb of the United States, beholden to their currency and their sanctions for far too long now. I truly believe this is our chance to sever that trend. . ."

Alex had one of his trusted financial advisors, a young Russian named Nikolai Breznev, who attended the Moscow Institute of Physics and Technology explain to him the concept of 'stock to flow'[5] with the help of the following chart one day and it was then the light clicked on for him:

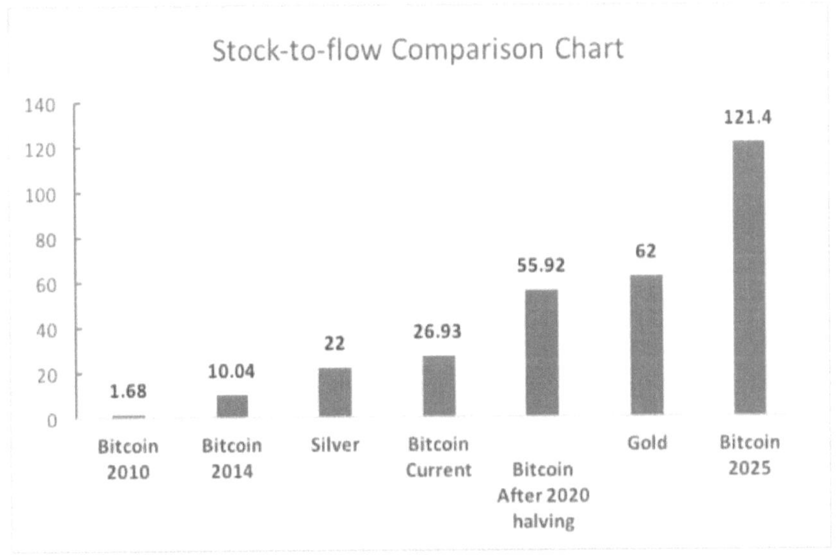

Source - ZPX, Satoshi&Co research

Alex knew and understood gold and the power of the dollar.

From that point forward, Alex used this chart as a bludgeoning instrument with his staff, including Sergey.

Sergey's hypothesis had developed into this: the survival of Russia's economic system, the leadership team and *possibly even the state of Mother Russia herself*, hinged on the accumulation of this strange currency.

He knew they were in an invisible race, an invisible poker match with the Chinese and the North Koreans, both of which he needed but neither of whom he trusted.

And then, of course, there were the Americans.

These *corporate peasants*, as he liked to call them, often with a smirk on his face, were publicly announcing their purchases in what he considered to be an irrationally bombastic manner. This was beginning to evoke the eyebrow raise from Alex . . .

Announcing their purchases??! Sergey thought, blood coursing through his veins. *How pathetically WEAK!??*

Sergey had speculated over the last two decades what happened to those people within their circle who received the eyebrow raise from Alex. Truth be told, Sergey had not actually seen what had happened to them; there was in fact, nothing to see. They would simply disappear, and a replacement would magically appear in the missing's place soon thereafter. No one dared to ask any questions, they simply *assumed*.

This morning, Sergey turned to his wingman Orgoff Balishikov and said:

"Can you believe these poisonous little dwarves? These idiots actually broadcast what they are buying because they are required to by their mindless *reporting* laws!" his veins gently bulging on his reddened temples.

He went on . . .

"It's a brilliant move by the U.S. government to control and force this disclosure. This way, at least the government knows what their corporate peasants are up to . . ."

He went on to explain to Orgoff: "Think about a poker match, Orgo, to use the West's vernacular . . . If you know the hand of half of your table, in this case, these *corporate peasants*, does that not afford you a strategic advantage? OF COURSE, IT

DOES!!!" He answered loudly, chortling without so much as giving the slow-moving Orgo a chance to respond.

His face quickly shifted.

Sergey continued in a crazed whisper, hissing, eyes glowing maniacally: "Fortunately for us, we play at NO such table and are under no such constraint. So to that, I say to HELL WITH THEM ALL and let them all die a slow and agonizing death. I swear by Mother Russia, they will never know what we are doing until it is too late . . ."

Orgo could see the red rage and deep fear in his boss's eyes, and now, he too was fearful.

CHAPTER 7

SANCTION BUSTING: PYONGYANG, NORTH KOREA

Democratic People's Republic of Korea (DPRK)

Jung Song Dong Central District

Kim Jung June, President of the Democratic People's Republic of Korea (DPRK) was grateful for another $350 billion, funneled indirectly from his enemy, the United States of America, into one of DPRK's secure accounts. Yes, indirectly in return for which they promised with crossed fingers to continue tapping the brakes on their nuclear weapons development program.

The brutal food shortages continued, and June's senior lieutenants were becoming increasingly concerned about the general commoner uprising they feared would ensue. The sanctions placed upon them by the United States were crippling them and they all knew it.

Snapping him from his deep thoughts, the Finance Minister, Ko Tong Jom, flanked by the Defense Minister, General Kim Jong-swan of the Peoples Republic of Korea walked into his office and asked the question very short, very brief:

"Follow protocol?"

DPRK officials knew that South Korea (SOKO), China and the United States were always listening, so they spoke with a cryptic, coded language and never said exactly what they meant and never under any circumstance vocalized the specific chess moves they were making.

The public firing squad was the end result for anyone who made that mistake, as the paranoid regime always assumed treason.

The *protocol* to which the finance minister was referring was an immediate purchase of a large tranche of Bitcoin with those 'indirect' funds. Their definition of indirect included employing ransomware, cyber thievery and other wickedly cool tools at their disposal because the United States of America certainly was not on the open market forum readily promoting the delivery of aid to this *terrorist nation-state* as the U.S. referred to them.

DPRK cyber technicians had figured out a way on the blockchain to make it look as if multiple 'whales' (large purchasers of Bitcoin) were acting on it at various points around the globe so as not to draw attention to North Korea (NOKO).

The DPRK Premier's sister, Sung Ta, a breathtakingly beautiful but ruthlessly evil human being (a small circle of advisors questioned whether she was truly human) ran all internal affairs and also decided who would go missing if they so much as looked a peculiar way or carried themselves in an unsuitable manner as they entered the room.

Turning toward the finance and defense ministers, slight smile on her face, Sung Ta said in her cold, ominous tone:

"It is time . . ."

CHAPTER 8
THE GRAVEST THREAT: ZHONGNANHAI, CHINA

Central HQ for the Chinese Communist Party (CCP) and the State
Council, Central Government

Li Quinping, President of the People's Republic of China (PRC) sat at the center of the circle of his counsel of 12 as he listened to his head of Intelligence (aptly named 'Ministry of State Security' or MSS) explain how they managed to track the probable whereabouts of Satoshi Nakamoto, the programmer who was the brainchild behind the creation of this dangerously *corrupt Bitcoin.*

Much of the world thought Nakamoto was a fictitious character or group of characters . . .

President Li knew as fact Nakamoto was one brilliant man at one point surrounded by very brilliant people. From his intelligence briefings, the President also knew that Nakamoto's actions were intentional. That is to say, Nakamoto understood as well if not better than the best experts in the world the concepts of 'exponential,' 'logarithmic growth' and 'stock-to-flow.' Nakamoto also understood avarice, fear, deceit, ruthlessness and the thirst some had for power. Like a world-class Jiu-Jitsu fighter, Nakamoto was adept at using his opponent's tendencies against him. In this case, *opponents* were a few select *nation*-states.

President Li felt a bit like one of the victims in this Jiu-Jitsu match and it did not sit well with him.

It was clear by Nakamoto's ghost-in-the-night-type vanishing, he understood that anyone who comes in the way of or even brushes up against dictatorial regimes and their power-thirsty leaders, with the mere threat of disrupting their power structure, was awarded an express ticket visit by the *angel of death.*

President Li desperately wanted to be that angel of death for Satoshi Nakamoto and demonstrate the extent of his ruthlessness.

How dare this Nakamoto create such poison? he thought.

As Mr. Nakamoto was kind enough to give the world the Genesis block, the MSS showed a rare obligatory sense of humor when they launched 'Operation Genesis.' Only this operation was not to facilitate a beginning—but an ending.

The Ministry of State Security always followed strict security protocols for their operations. This was now further emphasized due to information procured from their Russian Allies, vis-à-vis former U.S. Intelligence analyst and citizen named Eric Snakeden, with his fleeing of U.S. extradition. Comrade Snakeden was now granted *permanent resident* status in Russia, after being accused by the U.S. Government of providing aid and comfort to the enemy and deemed to be in violation of his nondisclosure agreement (Standard Form 312). As it turns out, Mr. Snakeden had provided invaluable and detailed information to Russia and China on how the NSA (National Security Agency) works and tracks information.

Thanks to Mr. Snakeden, the Chinese now knew more than ever about how America and its NSA employ their 'eyes and ears around the world.'

Under Operation Genesis, Satoshi Nakamoto's call name became *Fox One.*

Why *Fox One?* Nakamoto was also on China's non-public most wanted list, named "Operation Fox Hunt."[6][7] Fox Hunt is an espionage operation that was launched by the Chinese in June 2014. The covert operation was originally aimed at pursuing corrupt Chinese officials and business executives who fled abroad. However, as the Federal Bureau of Investigation Director mentioned in a speech at the Hudson Institute in New York in 2020: ". . . Fox Hunt is a sweeping bid . . . to target Chinese nationals who he sees as threats and who live outside of China across the world . . . We're talking about political rivals, dissidents and critics seeking to expose China's extensive human rights violations."

Though Nakamoto was not a Chinese National, Mr. Li and his trusted, airtight circle felt strongly that what he created in BTC posed a threat to China's stability. For this reason, capture and punishment was the only choice.

Operation Genesis gave the MSS much greater latitude on how to pursue and handle the *Fox One problem.*

For seven years the Chinese had pieced together intelligence on Fox One's whereabouts and believed him to be on an island just south of Tahiti. It was the largest island of the Windward group of the Society Islands in French Polynesia, located in the central part of the Pacific Ocean. The South Pacific. This is where their informant told them they would find Fox One.

Once captured, Fox One would be given a choice: A) he would either help the Chinese solve the riddle of the blockchain, that is: how to remove the cap of 21,000,000 coins Fox One had algorithmically programmed in; OR B) Fox One would suffer a fate worse than death for as long as they could keep him alive. Because the Ministry of State Security projected Fox One would willingly endure this fate, the same fate would befall whichever of Fox One's family members they could find and drag in front of him to demonstrate the same, providing him with an impressive, front-row seat to the lower levels of Hell.

They were waiting for the perfect time to send in their special forces group (namely the China Navy Jiaolong or "Sea Dragon" which some compare to the United States NAVY SEALS[8]). They suspected Fox One was ready to slip their noose and had sophisticated plans to evade capture or possibly trigger a suicidal event if so much as the breeze blew in an incorrect or unexpected pattern through the palm trees surrounding his hidden man-made created paradise.

Suicide was an event the Chinese simply could not allow.

As he thought about this, Li's smile broke and his thoughts shifted. He was furious that somehow a low-level intelligence officer in the United States Central Intelligence Agency had discovered not only their plot to *roll up* Fox One, but also their quiet accumulation of BTC through five different intermediaries around the globe. *How could this happen?*

"How had the U.S. managed to break our code?"

President Li had ordered a crackdown on all Bitcoin miners under the guise of protecting the people and the environment.

Li chuckled to himself, thinking *yes, protecting our minions and the environment. Just look at our Yangtze River.*

As he stared off to the far Lingshan mountain tops with a smiling rage he thought: *These idiots have no idea what they are doing or what they are talking about. Do they not understand what we are up against? We have to save these people from themselves. They are not smart enough to survive on their own . . .*

The news media was using the term 'crackdown' regarding the BTC mining incident, but rest assured, if it were being reported and had made the newswire, the brutality and ruthlessness of the ensuing 'crackdown' would be unfathomable. No doubt Bitcoin mines were having the plug pulled, but the dirty little fact was miners were also having their plug literally pulled, and were being quietly exterminated in normal, efficient fashion.

When officials of the PRC knock on your door, it's typically not a gracious courtesy call, not a pleasant first encounter.

One other inconvenient current event garnering Li's attention and fury was the fact a dear friend of his who had a young cousin, Wun Li, had suddenly gone missing. Wun Li was a cyber expert and blockchain whiz who was instrumental in hacking several different companies and who had storage houses for Bitcoin in the U.S.

With high probability, The Ministry of State Security narrowed down the kidnapping of his friend's cousin to the Mossad. In intel circles the Mossad was referred to as *The Institute,* meaning *Institute for Intelligence and Special Operations, the National Intelligence Agency of Israel, and* of course one of the staunchest allies of the United States.

Although considered a little brother to the U.S., this little brother was a ferocious tiger, a rattlesnake in the international community, not to be taken lightly by any country, no matter how large.

Li pondered: "If only we had such a valuable ally . . ."

If in the Mossad's grasp, Li assumed Wun Li was either dead or worse and much more likely, deep in the mountains of the western U.S. being tortured for information.

Li thought to himself: *This whole Bitcoin thing is a mess; it has become a major inconvenience, a thorn in our great country's side. We will either control it or eliminate those who stand in our way. Our long history has shown that sometimes we have to go to war to defend the proper way forward.*

CHAPTER 9

OPERATION IRON EAGLE: THE DISTRICT OF COLUMBIA

1500 Pennsylvania Avenue, NW – United States Department
of the Treasury

Janice Belton, Secretary of the Treasury of the United States of America, had done her level best in a strategic way of putting on a feigned campaign to talk BTC down to the markets. The ultimate poker match.

She could hear her former boss, Harvard Professor of Finance and onetime Chief advisor to the President of the United States saying: "Don't let the other side catch even a whiff of what you are doing as their sniffer is strong and if they smell that you are doing it, well, then the jig is truly up . . ."

Madam Belton along with the Federal Reserve Chairman Michael Hitchey and their staffs had run the numbers to understand what a flight from the U.S. dollar or gold or both to BTC would do to worldwide currency destabilization. They both never dared vocalize this, but they quietly feared that the U.S. dollar could lose its world reserve currency status. The nightmare scenarios emanating from this potential lost status as projected by their intelligence, economic and military teams were almost unspeakable.

Belton had warned Hitchey about the historic rate at which the Fed was printing money. Inflation was also at historic highs in the U.S. Unlike BTC, there was no limit to printing U.S. dollars and thus there was no limit to how diluted the currency could become. The U.S. was walking an economic tightrope, staring deep down into the abyss and they both knew it. And now, this "bitcoin thing."

After September 11, 2001, because of the unconventional nature of the attacks, The Central Intelligence Agency determined that alternate or unconventional thinking and preparation would need to be employed to help connect future dots and prevent such horrific occurrences. Some posited that had this kind of alternate or unconventional thinking been employed, the events of that catastrophic day may have been avoided.

As a result, the CIA formed the *Red Cell.*[9] Part of the Red Cell's mission was to derive nightmare, worst-case scenarios and more importantly to ensure that a 9/11-type event never happened again.

George Tenet, the Director of Intelligence who was in charge of the CIA at the time of 9/11, touched on it in his book *At the Center of the Storm: My Years at the CIA.*[10]

Taking a page from Red Cell, the Treasury and the Federal Reserve had formed a task force to produce worst-case scenarios and had granted this task force tip of spear capability.

If needed in the extreme case, the newly formed team would have instant access to the 'reach out and tap' resources of the Defense Department's Special Operations Command, which is to say Delta (officially known as 1st Special Forces Operational Detachment-Delta or 1st SFOD-D), SEALS and other special groups for immediate deployment.

This new task force was called 'Operation Iron Eagle.'

The two primary agencies on this task force were the Treasury and the Federal Reserve; the two primary supporting 'agencies' were the Defense Department and the CIA. So therein was the financial and economic brainpower, added to that, the Defense Department and Central Intelligence Agency which would provide the needed 'reach' or enforcement arm to *reach out and tap* whoever needed to be tapped. And rest assured, when Navy SEALS tap someone, that someone knows they have been tapped.

Iron Eagle was considered extremely sensitive and was placed in the category of *shoring up national security risk.* This is to say it had been determined that this phenomenon, this economic storm on the horizon, if it went 'the wrong way' (i.e., *not favoring the United States)* posed what the U.S. National Security Community deemed to be an unacceptable and extreme national security risk.

The United States government classification system is established under Executive Order 13526 which was signed into law by President Barack Obama, December 29, 2009.[11]

In the U.S., information is labeled 'classified' if it has been assigned one of the three levels:

1) Confidential, 2) Secret, or 3) Top Secret.

Iron Eagle was classified *Top Secret.*

Ms. Belton had just come out of another news briefing where she called Bitcoin 'inefficient' and voiced concern over 'illicit transactions.' This was a drum the Treasury Secretary had effectively been beating consistently over the previous two years or so. Many retail investors, otherwise known as small investors, tend to view leaders with admiration and trust if not a touch of skepticism and assume they normally have their best interests in mind. Often, these leaders actually do have good intentions; in some cases, they do not. It can be conditional.

In this case more retail investors coming into a market when there is a known finite supply was deemed troublesome, to say the least, and disastrous in its worst case. Especially if that *market,* in this case, BTC, has the potential of usurping the U.S. dollar as the world's reserve currency.

We can't have normal people acquiring this much power in terms of their financial independence, a cadre in the inner circle within the District thought; talk about the earth tilting and spinning backwards on its axis?

Well-respected private and publicly traded financial institutions had underwritten Bitcoin at $450,000 on a per coin basis today.

"This is getting out of hand. Those idiots actually said it aloud," Ms. Belton popped off to her staff one morning as she stormed out of her office in the Treasury building, red-faced, moving surprisingly briskly down the hall.

Truth be told these financial experts had actually underwritten it at a much higher level, but they were playing their own poker game.

When acquiring short positions or taking just about any position in the market most veteran investors do not reveal their hand. Those institutional *poker players,* some of the most brilliant financial and math minds in the world, always try to keep their eye on the 10,000-pound gorillas in the room, otherwise known as *Governments.* These collective financial institutions constantly attempt to do their best 'positing' as to which direction these 10,000-pound sovereign gorillas are or will be marching. This is due mainly to the fact that at the end of the day, the government can suck the air out of the entire world economic room.

See the Greek Government debt crisis in 2009 (widely known in Greece as 'The Crisis') as a small example of what can happen when even a minor economic global player has a hiccup.

The havoc and lurching it can cause in the gears of the entire economic 'Middle Earth' can be quite breathtaking.

Greece required bailout loans in 2010, 2012 and 2015 from the International Monetary Fund, Eurogroup and European Central Bank with Big Brother U.S. watching with a wary eye.

Financial institutions know that if the government, which can also be compared to that of a whale, rolls over on you, even if innocently while you are swimming aside it, it could kill you. So, you have to be wary at all times as to where the whales and gorillas are and what they are up to.

Corporation purchasing power for a balance sheet is one thing; the purchasing power of the Government whales is an exponentially different phenomenon altogether.

The ante at the world economic poker table goes WAY up when Governments come in; the institutional poker players know this and are often more agile and quicker to the table than these sovereign entities, thus where part of their financial success, on the margin, originates.

These institutions then attempt to ride the wave, sometimes a tsunami, created by the whales.

Madam Belton continued her brisk walk, now seeing the sunlight coming through the expansive doors of the U.S. Treasury Building. Navigating out of the building always seemed to be a longer walk than bridging the gap between the Treasury building and her destination, 1600 Pennsylvania Avenue, as it literally was right across the lawn.

To say the Treasury Secretary was not looking forward to the meeting with her boss, the President of the United States and the Joint Chiefs of Staff would be an understatement.

Ms. Belton thought of the briefing she received from her staff earlier in the day and her eyes squinted.

Of late, some unusual military movement and financial transactional activity were beginning to take place in areas around the globe that caused the Pentagon, The U.S. Treasury Department and the CIA serious concern. The U.S. Intelligence Community had determined the root cause of this activity was Bitcoin. Operation Iron Eagle appeared to be poised for takeoff.

Secretary Belton thought:

When you are standing on the beach and you look out and see the tsunami coming, the time for running has long since passed.

You better be a darn good swimmer.

CHAPTER 10

TSUNAMI ON THE HORIZON: NEW YORK, NEW YORK

Dano had touched down in the Big Apple five hours ago and had gotten to The Plaza Hotel where he would be staying for the next couple of nights, unpacked, showered up and took an hour nap. The 12-hour time difference always tossed his bios out of rhythm for about a day or so.

He had a meeting at 33 Liberty St. early the next morning which is home to the Federal Reserve Bank of New York.

He was hoping the Fed Bank of NY's staff leadership he would be meeting with would have answers for him. The public face the Fed and Treasury were putting on did not seem to be matching appropriately with the actions he was seeing, were counter to what his sources had been feeding him and he was now very frustrated.

Treasury Secretary Belton was flying in to attend the meeting.

Threats and blackmail were not his style. He once had a boss who would say regularly: "In God we Trust, everybody else better bring facts and data."

Dano had some facts and data he was prepared to lay down on the table for the Treasury Secretary and the Fed's staff. He was livid as he felt he had been lied to several times now. He had sent word to Belton's staff that multiple independent reliable sources confirmed to the World Business Journal that left no doubt: despite all of the public denials, his sources confirmed the U.S. was involved in the "quiet significant accumulation of a certain asset."

He had continued to play nice, but he was quickly tiring of the cat and mouse game with them and knew as well as anyone how to play hardball with bureaucrats when needed.

Dano made it clear he was prepared to kick the first stone to initiate the avalanche.

He thought:

Black mail? Last time I checked, blackmail was illegal, so no. A threat? Some may take it that way, but no. Facts and data and a little hardball? Absolutely.

There were some happenings that needed 'splaining as things simply were not adding up. There is a tsunami on the horizon . . .

The pace of economic and more menacingly military activity with the U.S., China, Russia and North Korea and their respective allies had picked up significantly.

He had a few questions that revolved around the apparent benevolent concerns for money laundering, terrorist financing and the like via Bitcoin. Curious still was the Treasury's interest in hiring and deploying 80,000 new IRS agents coming out of this global pandemic.

Good use of your taxpayer's dollars? he thought…

Dano and his colleagues had read the fine print in the Congressional Budget Office's (CBO) Report and had already formulated the series of questions.

Most understand the importance of prudent regulation, but governmental overreach is a separate matter altogether.

The moment the Treasury Secretary mentioned concern BTC's primary purpose would be for money laundering, financing terrorist groups and dark web transactions, Dano looked around the room and saw his colleagues in the press corps exchanging smirks.

The issues raised by the Secretary were issues they knew would generate public outcry, as of course they should, if they held true.

Dano had done his research.[12] [13] Several of the points being put forward as fact about BTC, many of which the Treasury Secretary was now espousing, had been debunked, including:

1) Digital currencies are primarily used for "dark" or illicit activity.
2) Bitcoin is not secure.
3) Bitcoin is a Ponzi scheme.
4) Bitcoin is anonymous (great for money laundering).

5) Bitcoin is bad for the environment.

In God we Trust, everybody else better bring facts and data. . .

He and his colleagues understood that part of the role of a Treasury Secretary or Finance Minister for any nation state, was to protect the value of its currency. Horrific implications awaited for those governments who did not do so.

As he looked out to Central Park South, a view he always cherished, he mumbled quietly, cheekbones tense: *A few questions indeed . . .*

EPILOGUE: LET IT BEGIN . . . LET IT END . . .: SOMEWHERE IN THE SOUTH PACIFIC OCEAN

Fox One, sitting on his teak palm tree ensconced balcony fortress, looked up from his iPad edition of the South China Morning Post and took in the sweeping, breathtaking views of the South Pacific.

Taking a small sip of green tea from his hand-crafted mug, he looked down to his left and saw the pelicans achieve liftoff in the distance.

He was smiling slightly as the breeze gently blew the palm tree leaves in a perfectly predictable, circular fashion.

Squinting through the sunlight dancing off the water, he spotted what looked to be the first signs of a small squall on the horizon . . .

His smile broadened.

At long last, a pathway to freedom, freedom for all. No more tyranny.

Yes, the economic atom had been split. The world war over Bitcoin had quietly begun and only God knew where it would go.

Let it Begin . . . Let it End . . .

ACKNOWLEDGMENTS

With every effort and crossed finish line I have had in my life, whether it is a marathon, or a business deal or whatever the case may be, when I looked back at the "game film" in the after, I realized someone, somewhere along the way helped me cross the finish line. Of course, I had to put forth my own energy and effort, but someone, somewhere along the way helped me. This has certainly been the case with my first fiction novelette, *World War Bitcoin*.

Thank you sincerely to all who helped me cross this finish line in my life…

I want to give a special thanks to the team who helped me edit and assemble this book, my awesome editor, Johanna Petronella Leigh, my reviewers, my awesome production designer, Ammad Zulfiqar and my adept technical advisor, John Frandano, and all who bore with me and helped me get it the way I wanted it.

And of course, to my family, friends and loved ones who supported me yet again.

I am forever grateful for all . . .

What a ride!

<h1 style="text-align:center">ENDNOTES:</h1>

Chapter 2

i.   Bitcoin: A Peer-to-Peer Electronic Cash System; Satoshi Nakamoto
      Nakamoto, Satoshi. *Bitcoin: A Peer-to-Peer Electronic Cash System*. PDF.

ii.   The Three Meanings of E= mc^2, Einstein's Most Famous Equation;
      Ethan Seigel; January 23, 2018; *Forbes*
      Seigel, Ethan. "The Three Meanings of E=mc^2, Einstein's Most Famous
      Equation." *Forbes, January 23, 2018. https://www.forbes.com/sites/
      startswithabang/2018/01/23/the-three-meanings-of-emc2-einsteins-most-
      famous-equation/?sh=435b478a71c0 Accessed November 8, 2021*

iii. The Times 03 Jan 2009
      "Bitcoin Genesis Block Newspaper - The Times 03 Jan 2009." *Genesis Block
      Newspaper - Copies of The Times Jan 3 2009*, https://www.thetimes03jan2009.
      com/. Accessed 8 Nov. 2021.

iv.   Absolute credit where credit is due here: This litmus test is actually part of
      MicroStategy's (listed on NASDAQ: MSTR; a real company and leader in the
      enterprise analytics world) and their CEO Michael Saylor's "Bitcoin" playbook
      –interview your author listened in on was on CNBC's "Squawk on the Street",
      November 1, 2021.
      MicroStrategy CEO's Bitcoin Playbook. www.youtube.com, https://www.youtube.
      com/watch?v=WiVh-59dN6w. Accessed 8 Nov. 2021.

Chapter 6

v.   A beginner's guide to the Bitcoin stock-to-flow model; Cointelegraph
      "A Beginner's Guide to the Bitcoin Stock-to-Flow Model." *Cointelegraph*, https://
      cointelegraph.com/trading-for-beginners/a-beginners-guide-to-the-bitcoin-
      stock-to-flow-model. Accessed 8 Nov. 2021.

Chapter 8

vi. All you need to know about China's Espionage programme 'Operation Fox Hunt'; Wion Web Team; July 8, 2020; *Wionews*
"All You Need to Know about China's Espionage Programme 'Operation Fox Hunt.'" *WION*, https://www.wionews.com/world/all-you-need-to-know-about-chinas-espionage-programme-operation-fox-hunt-311547. Accessed 8 Nov. 2021.

vii. China's Hunt for Dissidents has Gone Global; Hal Brands; September 12, 2021; *Bloomberg Opinion*
Brands, Hall. "China's Hunt for Dissidents Has Gone Global." *Bloomberg*, October 12, 2021. Accessed November 08, 2021. https://www.bloomberg.com/opinion/articles/2021-09-12/china-s-operation-fox-hunt-for-dissidents-includes-u-s-and-europe.

viii. How China's special forces stack up against the US's Special Operators; Stavros Atlamazoglou; Inside; December 1, 2020
Atlamazoglou, Stavros. "How China's Special Forces Stack up against the US's Special Operators." *Business Insider*, https://www.businessinsider.com/how-china-special-forces-compare-to-us-special-operators-2020-12. Accessed 8 Nov. 2021.

Chapter 9

ix. Inside the Red Cell; Micah Zenko; Excerpt in Foreign Policy; October 30, 2015 (Adapted from *Red Team: How to Succeed by Thinking Like the Enemy, by* Micah Zenko*)*
Zenko, Micah. "Inside the CIA Red Cell." *Foreign Policy*, https://foreignpolicy.com/2015/10/30/inside-the-cia-red-cell-micah-zenko-red-team-intelligence/. Accessed 8 Nov. 2021.

x.   At the Center of the Storm: My Years at the CIA; George Tenet with Bill Harlow; April 7, 2007
Tenet, George, and Bill Harlow. *At the Center of the Storm: My Years at the CIA.* Harper Collins, 2007.

xi. The President Executive Order 13526 ; *National Archives*; December 29, 2009. https://www.archives.gov/isoo/policy-documents/cnsi-eo.html ; *National Archives*; December 29, 2009

Chapter 10

xii. The 9 Biggest Bitcoin Myths That Need to be Debunked; Sylvain Saurel; January 7, 2020; *Medium.com*
Saurel, Sylvain. "The 9 Biggest Bitcoin's Myths That Need To Be Debunked." *The*

Startup, 7 Jan. 2020, https://medium.com/swlh/the-9-biggest-bitcoins-myths-that-need-to-be-debunked-d8dde3cb7a83. Accessed 8 Nov. 2021.

xiii. Top Bitcoin Myths Debunked; Nathan Reiff; Updated February 2, 2021; *Investopedia*
Reiff, Nathan. "Top Bitcoin Myths Debunked." *Investopedia*, https://www.investopedia.com/tech/top-bitcoin-myths/. Accessed 8 Nov. 2021.

ABOUT THE AUTHOR:

Pete has a combined 30+ years in the Fortune 500 supply chain and real estate arenas. As a former Fortune 500 Logistics/Supply Chain Exec who bounced all over the globe for quite a few years, after being diverted to Syracuse, NY en route from Boston's Logan Airport to Pittsburgh on a business trip that beautiful, fateful fall morning of September 11, 2001 (9/11) Pete decided to make a "right turn" in his life and pursue his small business ownership dreams in the real estate industry and more time with his family.

Pete takes considerable pride in having been called a "thought leader" by industry peers and has been fortunate to be recognized by his peers in leadership in the industry.

Pete is proud to be a small business owner and entrepreneur and has been the grateful recipient of a great deal of help along his journey. He enjoys nothing more than helping others run from peak to peak, to cross their finish lines.

Pete is a Bitcoin enthusiast, a big believer in the American Dream and because of his sons, has been honored with the best two words he feels he has ever been called:

Coach and Dad.